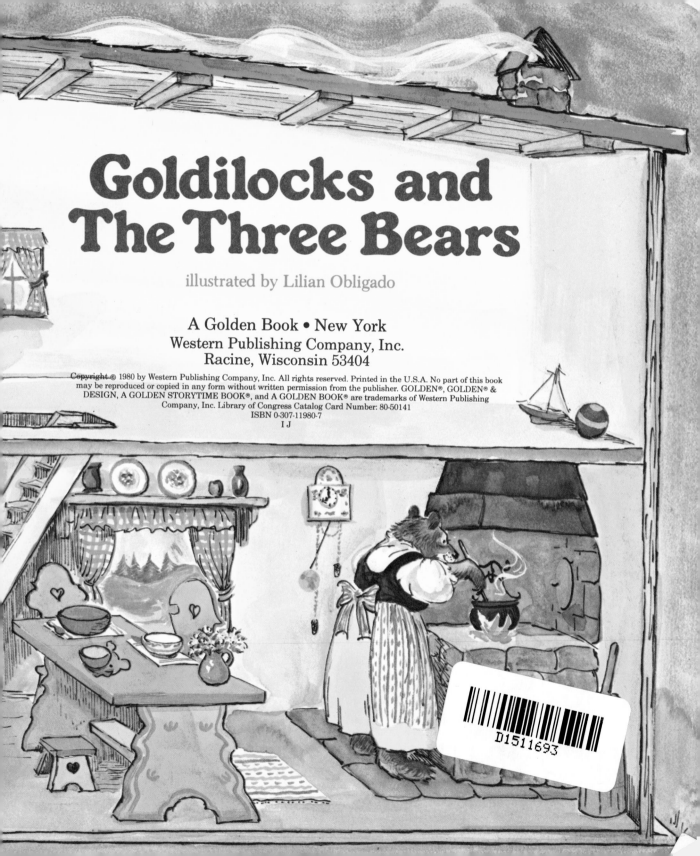

Goldilocks and The Three Bears

illustrated by Lilian Obligado

A Golden Book • New York
Western Publishing Company, Inc.
Racine, Wisconsin 53404

Copyright © 1980 by Western Publishing Company, Inc. All rights reserved. Printed in the U.S.A. No part of this book may be reproduced or copied in any form without written permission from the publisher. GOLDEN®, GOLDEN® & DESIGN, A GOLDEN STORYTIME BOOK®, and A GOLDEN BOOK® are trademarks of Western Publishing Company, Inc. Library of Congress Catalog Card Number: 80-50141
ISBN 0-307-11980-7
I J

Once upon a time there were three bears who lived in a cozy house in the woods. One was a great big papa bear, one was a middle-sized mama bear, and one was a little wee baby bear.

Each one had a bowl for porridge—a great big bowl for the papa bear, a middle-sized bowl for the mama bear, and a little wee bowl for the baby bear.

Each bear had a chair to sit in—a great big chair for the papa bear, a middle-sized chair for the mama bear, and a little wee chair for the baby bear.

And each bear had a bed to sleep in—a great big bed for the papa bear, a middle-sized bed for the mama bear, and a little wee bed for the baby bear.

One morning, the bears made porridge for their breakfast
and poured it into their bowls. Then they went out into
the woods for a walk while the porridge was cooling.

While they were away, a little girl named Goldilocks
passed by the house and looked in the window. Then she
peeped in the keyhole. Seeing nobody in the house, she
lifted the latch and went in.

Goldilocks should have waited until the bears came home. But since she was a naughty, greedy little girl, she set about helping herself to the porridge.

First she tasted the porridge in the great big bowl, but it was too hot.

Next she tasted the porridge
in the middle-sized bowl, but it
was too cold.

When she tasted the porridge
in the little wee bowl it was neither
too hot nor too cold, but just right.
And she liked it so much that she
ate it all up, every bit!

By this time Goldilocks was tired, so she sat down
to rest in the great big chair. But it was too hard.

Next she sat down
in the middle-sized chair.
But it was too soft.

When Goldilocks sat down in the little
wee chair it was neither too hard
nor too soft, but just right.

But she was so heavy that the chair
broke all in pieces. Down she came,
plump on the floor, and that made her
very cross!

Next Goldilocks went upstairs to the attic where the three bears slept. First she lay down on the great big bed. But it was too hard.

Then she lay down on the middle-sized bed.
But it was too soft.

At last she lay down on the little wee bed
and it was neither too hard nor too soft, but
just right. So she covered herself and fell
fast asleep.

By this time the three bears thought that their porridge must be cool, so they came home to eat breakfast. As soon as they walked into the house they could see that someone had been there.

"SOMEBODY HAS BEEN TASTING MY PORRIDGE!" said the papa bear in his great gruff voice.

"SOMEBODY HAS BEEN TASTING MY PORRIDGE!" said the mama bear in her middle-sized voice.

Then the baby bear cried in his little wee voice,

"SOMEBODY HAS BEEN TASTING MY PORRIDGE, AND HAS EATEN IT ALL UP!"

The three bears began to look around.
"SOMEBODY HAS BEEN SITTING IN MY CHAIR!"
said the papa bear in his great gruff voice.

"SOMEBODY HAS BEEN SITTING IN MY CHAIR!"
said the mama bear in her middle-sized voice.

"SOMEBODY HAS BEEN SITTING IN MY
CHAIR, AND HAS BROKEN IT ALL IN PIECES!"
cried the baby bear in his little wee voice.

Next the three bears decided to look upstairs in the attic.
"SOMEBODY HAS BEEN SLEEPING IN MY BED!"
said the papa bear in his great gruff voice.

"SOMEBODY HAS BEEN SLEEPING IN MY BED!"
said the mama bear in her middle-sized voice.

"SOMEBODY HAS BEEN SLEEPING IN MY BED!"
cried the baby bear in his little wee voice,
"AND HERE SHE IS!"

The little wee voice of the baby bear was so shrill that
Goldilocks woke up at once. When she saw the three bears she
tumbled out of bed, and fled downstairs and out the door.